Reading books toge   st pleasurable
activities you share with your   ldren love to
spend time with their parents, and   tunity to be the
focus of your undivided attention. To get the most out of
reading together, try to find a relaxed time that suits your
family. Remember, reading should be fun, so show your
enthusiasm and this will transfer to your child. If he or she is
wriggling away, leave it for another occasion.

First Time Stories show familiar situations from everyday
life that young children can relate to easily. Repetition helps
children understand, so I suggest you read this book together
more than once. You can use the story as a chance to talk about
similar situations in your own child's life. As you read, follow
the words with your finger to show the connection of the
written word to what you are saying. Enc   's
imagination if he or she wants to tell a   m
the pictures. Above all, enjoy reading toge

Eileen Hayes
Parenting Consultant to the NSPCC

FIRST TIME STORIES

We're Moving House

Heather Maisner

ILLUSTRATED BY Kristina Stephenson

KINGFISHER

I don't want to move house, Amy thought,
looking out of the window at the flowers she'd
planted with her dad and her best friend, Eve.
I'll miss Eve, and I'll miss the flowers.

Crash! Bang! Whack!

Behind her, Ben threw toy cars into a box, shouting, "We're off! We're off!" as he zoomed round the room.

"Time to go," said Mum, holding Figaro the cat.

The car was crowded. Figaro's cat box took up half the back seat. Eve ran up and thrust a blue, furry teddy bear into Amy's hands.

"Take this!" she said. And she waved and waved as the car drove off.

Amy cuddled the blue bear. Ben sang. Figaro miaowed and Dad drove for miles and miles.

The new house echoed. Men walked in and out, carrying boxes. There were no pictures on the walls or curtains at the windows, and the furniture stood higgledy-piggledy in the middle of each room.

Ben ran up and down the stairs, shouting, "Here we are! Here we are!"

The next day, Mum
was busy emptying boxes.
Dad was balanced on a
chair, fitting a lampshade.

The floorboards creaked and footsteps moved towards her. She was about to scream, when a little voice said, "Can I come in your bed? I don't like it on my own."

"Oh, all right," said Amy.

Ben climbed in beside her and Amy was secretly pleased.

That night, Amy lay in her bed feeling scared and lonely. In the old house, she had shared a room with Ben. The moon cast shadows through the window. A door rattled. Pipes gurgled and a car swooshed past down the road. Amy shivered. Then she heard a strange snivelling sound.

Amy stared out at the wild garden,
thinking, *There aren't any flowers.*

Ben couldn't find his favourite green toy car.
"I've left it behind," he wailed. "We have to go back."
"I'll help you look for it," said Amy.

Amy and Ben searched every room.
They found a dusty book in a cupboard . . .

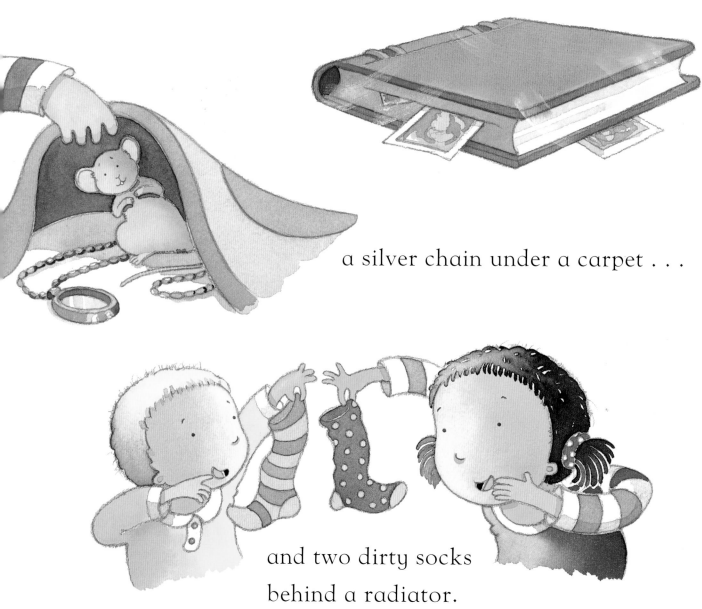

a silver chain under a carpet . . .

and two dirty socks
behind a radiator.

They crept downstairs to the cold, dark cellar. They found an old boot and lots of scurrying spiders, but they couldn't find the green car anywhere.

"Let's try the garden," said Amy.

They made a path through the weeds to an
overgrown pond. A frog jumped into the water
with a plop. Birds fluttered and squawked.
Figaro sat on his haunches, staring over the tall
grass. Ben found a rope swing hanging from
a tree, and Amy swung high into the sky.

Splattered with mud, they
ran back into the house.

"Take off your shoes,"
Mum shouted as they
raced upstairs.

Amy's room looked completely different. It had
curtains and a rug, and all her teddy bears sat in a
row on the bed, just like they did in the old house.

Amy slid her feet into her slippers, but she couldn't get one on. She frowned and bent down. Ben's favourite green car was hiding inside.

"I've found it," she called. "I've found it!"

The next day,
they went shopping.
Amy chose pink
and purple paint
for her room.

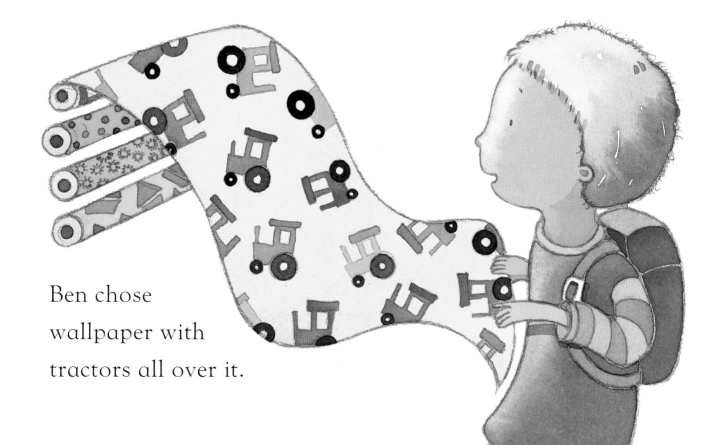

Ben chose
wallpaper with
tractors all over it.

Mum bought everything in yellow for the kitchen.
Dad bought a drill and a new set of tools.
They walked back to the car with their packages.

Suddenly, Amy stopped in front of a garden centre.
Dad bumped into her, almost dropping his packages.

"What is it?" he asked. "What's wrong?"

But Amy didn't answer. She couldn't. She bit her lip hard,
to hold back the tears.

Dad looked over his mountain of packages and said,
"Oops, there's something we've forgotten."

He hurried inside and came out with two trays of flowering plants, just like the ones they'd had at the old house.

"Thanks!" said Amy, jumping up to kiss him.

Later, Dad and Amy worked in the garden. A boy and a
girl leaned over the gate to watch.

"What are you doing?" asked the boy.

"Planting flowers," said Amy.

"Can we help?" asked the girl.

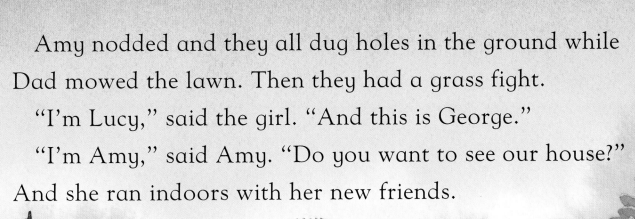

Amy nodded and they all dug holes in the ground while
Dad mowed the lawn. Then they had a grass fight.

"I'm Lucy," said the girl. "And this is George."

"I'm Amy," said Amy. "Do you want to see our house?"
And she ran indoors with her new friends.

The publisher thanks Eileen Hayes, Parenting Advisor to the NSPCC,
for her kind assistance in the development of this book.

For Rosie and Ruby – H.M.
For Maddie and Charlie – K.S.

KINGFISHER
An imprint of Kingfisher Publications Plc
New Penderel House, 283-288 High Holborn
London WC1V 7HZ
www.kingfisherpub.com

First published by Kingfisher 2004
2 4 6 8 10 9 7 5 3 1

Text copyright © Heather Maisner 2004
Illustrations copyright © Kristina Stephenson 2004

A CIP catalogue record for this book
is available from the British Library.

ISBN 0 7534 0997 6

Printed in Singapore
1TR/0704/TWP/PICA(PICA)/150MA